THE TOP JOB

BY

Elizabeth Cody Kimmel

ILLUSTRATED BY

Robert Neubecker

DUTTON CHILDREN'S BOOKS

To Marcia Wernick—who is always tops in my book
E.C.K.

To my excellent niece, Taylor
R.N.

DUTTON CHILDREN'S BOOKS
A division of Penguin Young Readers Group

Published by the Penguin Group
Penguin Group (USA) Inc., 375 Hudson Street, New York, New York 10014, U.S.A. · Penguin Group (Canada), 90 Eglinton Avenue East, Suite 700,
Toronto, Ontario, Canada M4P 2Y3 (a division of Pearson Penguin Canada Inc.) · Penguin Books Ltd, 80 Strand, London WC2R 0RL, England · Penguin Ireland,
25 St Stephen's Green, Dublin 2, Ireland (a division of Penguin Books Ltd) · Penguin Group (Australia), 250 Camberwell Road, Camberwell, Victoria 3124, Australia
(a division of Pearson Australia Group Pty Ltd) · Penguin Books India Pvt Ltd, 11 Community Centre, Panchsheel Park, New Delhi - 110 017, India · Penguin Group (NZ),
67 Apollo Drive, Mairangi Bay, Auckland 1311, New Zealand (a division of Pearson New Zealand Ltd) · Penguin Books (South Africa) (Pty) Ltd, 24 Sturdee Avenue,
Rosebank, Johannesburg 2196, South Africa · Penguin Books Ltd, Registered Offices: 80 Strand, London WC2R 0RL, England

LIBRARY OF CONGRESS CATALOGING-IN-PUBLICATION DATA

Kimmel, Elizabeth Cody.
The top job / Elizabeth Cody Kimmel ; illustrated by Robert Neubecker.   p. cm.
Summary: On Career Day, a young girl entertains the class with a description of her father's
exciting job as light bulb changer at the top of the Empire State Building.
ISBN: 978-0-525-47789-1 (hardcover)
1. Empire State Building (New York, N.Y.)—Juvenile fiction. [1. Empire State Building (New York, N.Y.)—Fiction.
2. Occupations—Fiction. 3. Fathers and daughters—Fiction.] I. Neubecker, Robert, ill. II. Title.
PZ7.K56475Top 2007   [E]—dc22   2006059770

Published in the United States by Dutton Children's Books,
a division of Penguin Young Readers Group
345 Hudson Street, New York, New York 10014
www.penguin.com/youngreaders
Designed by Sara Reynolds and Abby Kuperstock
Manufactured in China · First Edition
1 3 5 7 9 10 8 6 4 2

On Career Day, Mrs. Feeny asked her students to stand up in class and talk about their parents' jobs.

Emma Sweetpaw said her dad was a UFO hunter.
She said he used a two-ton telescope to search the sky for flying
saucers and a giant satellite to receive alien transmissions.

Elizabeth O'Malley asked if Emma's dad had introduced
her to any real, live space aliens.

She said no, but she did get to see a meteor shower.

Elizabeth O'Malley said her mom was a jeweler.
Elizabeth got to hold diamonds, rubies, and emeralds
while her mom made a tiara for the princess of Pollonico.

Aidan Drapersley asked if Elizabeth got to meet the princess.

She said no, but she did get to see a very pretty woman
trying on her engagement ring.

Aidan Draper said his mom was a NASCAR driver.
He went to the speedway and got to watch the race
from a special booth for Very Special People.

I asked Aidan if his mom let him try on the flameproof jumpsuit.

He said no, but he did get to wear her helmet on the way home.

When it was my turn, I stood up in front of the class and said that my dad changed lightbulbs.

Anthony Swister said, "Booooooring!" and laughed
so hard he popped the top button off his pants.

Mrs. Feeny told Anthony to put his head down on his desk.
Then she said we were out of time for Career Day talks,
and asked the class to get out *Spelling Is Spectacular.*

But I wasn't finished yet, so I didn't sit down
or get out my spelling book.
I stayed where I was and kept on talking.

I said that my dad had changed a lightbulb just last weekend.
He let me go along to help. We had to get up very early,
because it would take most of the day.

Then we took a bus,

a train,

and a subway
just to get to

the building where the lightbulb needed changing.

And getting to the building was only the beginning. I helped him
put on his work stuff next. Just the usual—

a hard hat with a
light attached,

leather gloves with
cutoff fingers,

a climbing harness,

a coil of
Manila safety rope,

sticky-bottomed climber's boots,

and coveralls with his name sewed right on the front. He had a
special bag clipped onto his harness to hold the new lightbulb.
It's about the size of our beagle's head but 620 watts brighter.

Next he had to get the lightbulb all the way
up to the building's tippy-top.
Everyone in my class started to look kind of interested,
so I kept right on talking.

I explained there was no ladder in the whole world big enough to
reach the top of this building. Dad and I took an elevator up as high
as it went—to the 102nd floor. But we still had a long way to go.

We walked to a special hatch.
We opened it up, and that's where I stayed.
I had a great view of the clouds from there.

But Dad went through the hatch to the outside of the building.
That's where the ladder is. I explained that only Extremely Special
and Important People are allowed to climb the ladder,
and I looked at Aidan when I said that.

I told the class that my job was to stay by the hatch and be the
lookout while Dad climbed. I looked out for anything that might
be important—like thunderstorms, or flocks of birds, or UFOs,
and I looked at Emma when I said that.

Dad climbed. And climbed. And climbed.

I said my dad had to be very strong and not afraid of heights.
That's because he had to climb to the very top of the ladder,
which is built onto a big antenna. The lightbulb went
on the tippy-top of the antenna.

Mrs. Feeny closed *Spelling Is Spectacular* and asked,
"Exactly how high is this tippy-top your dad has to get to?"

I whipped out my pocket calculator. I told Mrs. Feeny that the
ladder on the antenna went up for 117 feet. After that, Dad had to
climb right up the antenna itself, using little bolts to put his feet on.
But that was only for the last 87 feet. That makes 204 feet.
Plus those 102 floors we came up on the elevator.

I explained that's why I had brought my catcher's mitt, just in case.
Dad only had the one lightbulb with him, and if he dropped it
(I did a quick sum on the calculator) and I didn't catch it, it would
fall one thousand four hundred fifty-three feet and eight and
nine-sixteenths inches to the sidewalk.

So it probably would have broken.

Mrs. Feeny said, "Oh my goodness, I certainly hope
he climbed nice and slowly!"

I said no, as a matter of fact, he had to go pretty fast.
See, usually there's 17 million watts going through the
antenna for the TV stations and radio stations that use it
for their broadcasts. They have to shut them all down while
the lightbulb is being changed. And you know, I said, TV
and radio stations do not like to be shut down for very long.
Mrs. Feeny asked me to please continue.

So I said that by now the sun had set and the stars were coming
out. Dad and I were so high up in the sky the stars looked like
diamonds you could just reach out and grab.
I looked at Elizabeth when I said that.

And I mentioned that on the observation deck below, a whole crowd of tourists started cheering. They had been watching all along. Dad and I were used to that. He held on to the antenna with one hand and waved with the other. I held on to my catcher's mitt with one hand and waved with the other.

But by then there was no time to lose.
Dad took out the old lightbulb and pulled the new one
out of his special bag. We all held our breath.
He screwed in the new lightbulb one turn at a time.

THE EMPIRE STATE BUILDING WAS BACK IN BUSINESS!

Everyone was still cheering when my dad climbed back down the ladder and through the hatch. He told me the bulb would stay lit for two years before burning out. I said this was good news for birds and UFO pilots and King Kong, and anyone else who needed to see the tippy-top of this building in the dark.

Mrs. Feeny said, "Gracious, how exciting! Is there anything else?"

I explained that, just if anyone was interested, the antenna was originally supposed to be a mooring mast for airships called dirigibles. I told Mrs. Feeny she might want to look that word up in *Spelling Is Spectacular* and write it on the blackboard, since it's hard to spell.

I finished up by telling the class that after Dad climbed back down,
we went and had a hot dog at the snack bar.
Dad got me a T-shirt, too.

Mrs. Feeny said, "Do you think the class could go to work with you and your dad next weekend and watch him change another lightbulb?"

I told Mrs. Feeny that next weekend my dad wasn't going to change any lightbulbs. . . .

He was going to wash some windows instead.